To Leighton

Enid who? Enji

Dave

David MacGill

The author has worked in the finance industry for nearly 40 years and is married with two daughters and a son, all now adults, and two grandsons. The idea for the story book stemmed from the older grandson, Corey, who was seven at the time, stating that penguins and polar bears could never meet as they inhabited opposite poles. The author, therefore, decided to write a story for him whereby a penguin and a polar bear not only did actually meet, but subsequently became best friends. The author was born and lives in Edinburgh.

PARJITER PENGUIN'S AMAZING ARCTIC ADVENTURE

DAVID MACGILL

AUSTIN MACAULEY PUBLISHERS™

LONDON · CAMBRIDGE · NEW YORK · SHARJAH

A CIP catalogue record for this title is available from the British Library.

ISBN 9781398473447 (Paperback)
ISBN 9781398473454 (ePub e-book)

www.austinmacauley.com

First Published 2022
Austin Macauley Publishers Ltd®
1 Canada Square
Canary Wharf
London
E14 5AA

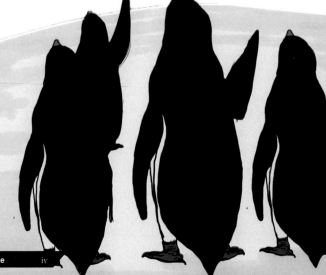

Dedicated to my two grandsons, Corey and Noah.
Corey's assertion that penguins and polar bears could
never meet as they inhabit opposite ends of the world,
was the inspiration to write a story that proved otherwise.

Chapter 1
End of Term

Primrose Penguin put her whistle to her beak and gave it a loud blast.

"Everyone in for lunch. Quickly now." Her shrill voice pierced the cold Antarctic air. "That means you as well, Parjiter."

Parjiter had, as usual, been daydreaming.

"Oh, sorry," said Parjiter rather quietly. "What are we having for lunch today, Miss Primrose?"

"Fish pie. I made it myself," she announced proudly.

"Why am I not surprised," muttered Parjiter to himself. "We have fish pie every day."

"Did you say something, Parjiter?"

"No, Miss Primrose," he replied, "it must have been the wind you heard."

Primrose Penguin gave Parjiter a knowing look and said, "Don't forget to wash your flippers before you eat."

Parjiter and his classmates sat down to lunch. Even though it was the same meal as they always had, it actually tasted very good.

"Most flavoursome, Miss Primrose," said Parjiter with a cheeky grin on his face.

After lunch all the young penguins filed into the classroom where Primrose Penguin (who was their teacher as well as lunch cook) made an announcement to the class.

"As you know," she started, "this is the last day of school term, and you will now be going off on holiday for three months until the worst of the winter is over."

There was a loud cheer from all the assembled penguins.

"But before you go," she continued, we have one final lesson."

Some of the penguins groaned. They wanted to leave for the winter holidays now.

"Now, you will remember that all of our lessons have been about our own lifestyle – how we are all members of a huge colony of Emperor Penguins who look after one another and try to protect each other from predators as best we can."

Parjiter knew only too well how dangerous life could be if you got careless. His daydreaming had nearly proved to be very costly on several occasions in the past when he had wandered off from the safety of the penguin colony, only to be targeted from the air by birds who were a danger, like giant petrels and skuas, just looking for a tasty penguin chick for dinner.

It was only due to the adult penguins rushing to his rescue that prevented Parjiter from being carried off in their claws, never to be seen again.

The danger was not just from the air, however. The sea could be just as perilous, as any penguins who were out catching fish, or even just going for a casual swim, had to have their wits about them and keep out of the way of leopard seals and killer whales. Getting too close to them was definitely not a good idea!

Parjiter snapped out of his personal thoughts as he realised that Miss Primrose was still addressing the class.

"Today, however," she continued, "I'm going to talk about life in the Arctic, which is as far away as you can get from where we all live, here in the south – in the Antarctic."

The young penguins gradually stopped muttering amongst themselves and gave the teacher their undivided attention. This was something very different from their usual lessons and they couldn't wait to hear about what life was like at the top end of the world.

The class sat in silence, soaking up all the knowledge that was being expertly imparted to them about how the Arctic also had ice caps and snow (although it was still considerably colder at the South Pole than it was at the North Pole), and how there were no penguins at all that lived up there.

The young students listened enthralled; however, Miss Primrose had saved the best till last.

"Finally," she said, with a glint in her eye, the largest animal that lives in the Arctic is the biggest of all species of bear, the Polar Bear, which can grow up to ten feet tall when standing on its hind legs."

Then, with a pause to let that startling piece of information sink in, she reached into her desk and produced a huge poster of a fully grown adult polar bear.

There were gasps of amazement from the class.

"Wow!" said one of the penguins. "How can anything grow that big?"

"That's awesome," said another.

Yet another remarked, "Thank goodness we don't have any polar bears down here in the Antarctic."

"That's very true," said Miss Primrose, "it's certainly a good thing that with polar bears living in the north and penguins living in the south, polar bears and penguins can never meet! We've got enough dangers to worry about without being chased by gigantic bears."

The young penguins burst into laughter, but Parjiter, who had been listening intently to this last amazing lesson of the term, was in no mood to laugh. Instead, he started to daydream again, and wondered what it would be like to come face to face with one of those big, furry white bears.

Miss Primrose wished all the young penguins in her class a good holiday, and reminded them to look out for each other and to stay safe.

"I'll see you all again in three months for the start of the new term," she said, and with these final words ringing in their ears, the youngsters waddled off and dispersed into the snow-covered sea ice.

Chapter 2
Parjiter Plans a Journey

The colony of Emperor Penguins were not alone in this natural sea-ice habitat. There were many human residents there as well, although they did not stay there all year round. These were the scientific researchers who had set up huge tents for living quarters while they studied the life cycle of the penguin colony and recorded any changes taking place in the massive glaciers which made up part of the penguins' home.

The penguin colony had become used to the humans living around them and actually regarded them as friends, as they were not there to cause them any harm. Quite the opposite, in fact, they were there to try and ensure that all the penguin colonies survived and did not have their habitat harmed by the effects of global warming.

The penguins quite happily used to wander in and out of the researchers' camp without being bothered. In fact, many of the researchers were constantly photographing the penguins as they waddled about the tents.

Parjiter liked posing for the photos as he could be a bit of a show-off. When he spotted the cameras being pointed in his direction, that was his cue to glide past them on one leg as if he was on ice skates and flap his flipper wings flamboyantly, before finishing off his performance with a spectacular pirouette.

This drew howls of laughter and a resounding cheer from his audience as Parjiter took a final bow, secure in the knowledge that he had produced yet another perfect show for the assembled masses.

Parjiter's exertions had left him exhausted, so he waddled over to one of the research tents and flopped down at the entrance to have a well-earned rest.

From inside the tent, Parjiter could hear the researchers discussing details of their next scientific expedition. As the discussion continued, their voices gradually became raised with excitement. Parjiter could now hear every detail of the expedition being planned.

"Travelling non-stop by ship from the Antarctic all the way up to the Arctic has never been done before," said one of the researchers. "Do you really think that we can do it?"

"Of course, we can," responded another.

"We've been studying the Emperor Penguins who, out of all the eighteen species of penguin in the world, are the largest and live the farthest south. Now we have a chance to study the largest of the eight different species of bear in the world and whose habitat is the farthest north – the Polar Bear!"

Parjiter suddenly sat bolt upright.

"Did he say they were going to study polar bears?" Parjiter said to himself.

After seeing the poster of the huge polar bear that Miss Primrose had shown to the class, Parjiter thought that it would have been awesome to go on that expedition all the way to the Arctic.

They are so lucky! he thought.

The researchers continued their discussion.

"We're all agreed then. We'll leave by ship tomorrow morning and cross the Drake Passage, which is only about six hundred miles of open sea, and then load up with supplies for our epic voyage," said the lead scientist.

"Where will we get the supplies?" enquired one of the team.

"We'll land at Ushuaia for some of the supplies and then pick up the rest at Puerto Williams which is only a few miles further on, before heading off north."

"What's the name of that place? Oosh something?"

"Ushuaia. It's pronounced Oos-wye-ah. Both that and Puerto Williams are the two most southerly cities in the world but they're really close to each other," the lead scientist explained. "And they're actually in different countries," he continued. "Ushuaia is at the southern tip of Argentina, and Puerto Williams is in Southern Chile."

The expedition leader then proceeded to detail the route that they would take for the approximate 8,000-mile voyage. They would head up through the Pacific Ocean hugging the west coast of the South American continent before passing through the Panama Canal and then entering the Caribbean Sea. From there, they would continue up through the North Atlantic Ocean until reaching Greenland, their final destination.

"Phew, that's some voyage. No wonder no one has attempted that before," said another of the research team. How long will the whole voyage take?"

The reply came, "We'll be on the open sea for about a month before we land in Greenland. Then we'll work on our polar bear research for a further month, before heading back to our research camp here in the Antarctic.

The journey back will take another month, of course, so we'll be away for three months in total."

"Right, guys, we've got an early start in the morning, so let's get some sleep. It's going to be a long day tomorrow."

Parjiter was, quite naturally, totally confused about all the planning, but one thing was certain. He had to find a way of sneaking aboard that ship. The more he thought about seeing a polar bear face to face, the more excited he became.

Parjiter rushed over to tell all of his friends about what he was planning to do.

"But you can't do that Parjy," said one. "What if you get caught?"

"I'll hide in the ship so that no one will see me," said Parjiter.

"It's a really long trip though. What will you eat?" asked another.

"I'm sure there will be food on the ship somewhere," he replied.

"But what if a polar bear eats you?"

Parjiter laughed. "Don't worry, I'm not planning on getting that close to one. I just want to actually see one for myself."

"How long will you be away for, Parjy?" asked another of his friends.

"Ah," said Parjiter, "that's the beauty of this voyage. I overheard the scientists saying it would take three months in total before they land back here again, which is exactly how long our school holidays last, so I'll be back just in time for the new term starting."

Parjiter seemed to have all the answers, so all that his friends could do was to wish him good luck and to have a safe journey.

Parjiter thanked them and wandered off to get some sleep before the big day in the morning.

"Now," said Parjiter to himself, "what was it that Miss Primrose said to the class? Ah, yes, 'Polar bears and penguins can never meet.'"

"Really! Well, we'll see about that."

Chapter 3
Preparations Concluded

Early next morning Parjiter awoke to the sound of tents and scientific equipment being packed away and wheeled up the research ship's gangplank to be stored for the duration of the voyage.

Now's my chance to sneak aboard, he thought.

As there was a steady stream of equipment being loaded on to the ship, Parjiter saw his opportunity. The next trolley to be taken on board contained two large crates and with just enough space in between them for a small penguin to squeeze into. When he was sure that no one was looking, he jumped on to the trolley.

Perfect fit, he thought, as he hid between the crates and was then wheeled up the gangplank and on to the deck of the ship. Just as carefully as he had boarded, he jumped off the trolley and scurried away out of sight.

"So far, so good. Now, where am I going to hide?"

Parjiter scanned the ship's deck until his gaze stopped abruptly, and a beaming smile played over his face.

A series of lifeboats lined the side of the ship.

That's it, Parjiter thought with a satisfied nod of his head. I'll hide in one of these little boats. No one will even bother looking in there. He settled down into his new quarters.

Later that morning Parjiter heard the sound of the engine starting up and felt the motion of the ship as it slowly moved away from the edge of the ice shelf. He took a deep breath and sneaked a peak from under the lifeboat's cover, only to see his home and his penguin colony disappearing into the distance as the ship gained speed and headed out into the open sea.

"Well, there's no going back now," he said to himself. I hope this whole thing isn't a big mistake."

"No, of course it's not!" Parjiter tried to reassure himself. "It's exactly what I want to do!"

As the journey across the Drake Passage continued, the sea became increasingly rough, and huge waves crashed against the ship as it ploughed its way towards the first port of call.

The steady sway of the ship had made Parjiter seasick. He had never been on a ship before and wasn't expecting to feel so unwell. He certainly didn't realise that the sea could be so rough. There was nothing that he could do about it, however, so he just had to think of something to take his mind off this ordeal.

"I wonder if polar bears get seasick too?" he pondered. "Imagine if a whole family of polar bears were on a boat trip, became seasick and were all lined up in a row, bent over the side of the boat being sick. What a sight that would be to see all those big furry bottoms sticking up in the air like a row of giant cotton wool balls. Now, that would be funny!"

The thought of that sight made Parjiter laugh to himself and was enough to make him forget, temporarily at least, about how seasick he was feeling.

As time passed, the heavy seas subsided until just a gentle swell remained as the ship sailed into the harbour for its first stop. This was the port of Ushuaia, and the ship's crew very quickly and efficiently loaded on board all the supplies that were needed for the journey north.

Parjiter watched all this activity from the safety of the lifeboat that he had made his temporary home, as extra scientific equipment was being carefully loaded on to the ship. The last object to be loaded on board was so large that it took ten of the crew to heave it slowly up the gangplank.

Parjiter was curious. What on earth was this huge metal container that was now being secured and bolted to the middle part of the ship's deck?

It must be really important, he thought, as the crew finished the job of fixing and fitting this strange object that was taking up so much space.

Soon, however, they were on their way again for the short trip along a narrow channel of water to the last stop before the main voyage. This was Puerto Williams.

Parjiter thought, Why on earth do they need more stuff for the journey? Haven't they got enough?

Then, when he saw what was now being loaded on board, Parjiter realised exactly why this was probably the most important stop, at least as far as he was concerned.

What seemed like an endless stream of crates containing many varieties of food supplies were being carried up the gangplank, but it was the final few crates which excited him the most, as these contained boxes of fresh fish.

The big metal doors of the mysterious container were opened and the food was deposited inside. Parjiter now realised what the container was for. It was a gigantic walk-in refrigerator which would allow the ship's crew to have fresh food for the duration of the month-long voyage to Greenland.

Chapter 4
Operation Arctic Commences

As the expedition ship sailed out of Puerto Williams harbour, it was cheered on loudly by the local people who waved and shouted their good luck messages to the crew on board, as they knew that a particularly momentous voyage was about to be embarked upon.

Very quickly the land was left far behind, and all that could now be seen was the massive expanse of the blue Pacific Ocean.

From horizon to horizon, this would be the only sight that would greet the crew for the next two weeks as the ship headed north, up past the entire west coast of the South American continent, on the first leg of the month-long voyage.

Meantime, as Parjiter hadn't eaten for a few days due to being seasick, he was now getting rather peckish and fancied something to eat. He hoped though, that the sea would remain much calmer so that he could at least enjoy his dinner.

Parjiter had noticed that the huge fridge doors were constantly being opened and shut, with food supplies frequently being taken out to feed the ship's crew.

So when the fridge doors were next opened up, Parjiter sneaked in and headed straight over to where the boxes of fish were being stored. He had never seen so many fish at the same time, and the great thing was, he didn't even have to try and catch them himself. They were all just lying there in rows ready to be eaten.

The fish were so numerous, in fact, that he knew that no matter how many he took, there was no way that they would ever be missed.

Parjiter had heard at school about how humans had to buy their food at places called supermarkets. They had to fill their baskets, then take the food home to eat it.

He had always thought that this was very odd, indeed, as all he had to do for a meal was to dive into the sea, catch some fish in his beak and then eat them. This was a much simpler process.

However, as he was travelling in a ship full of humans, he thought that, just for a bit of fun, he would do as they do.

So Parjiter grabbed an empty box that was lying nearby and skipped along the rows of fish, saying out loud, "Hmm, I'll have one of these, and one of those, and two of these, and oh, I like the look of those so I'll take half a dozen. Thank you very much."

Parjiter thought that this was hilarious. He filled his box and then had to stagger back to his lifeboat unseen, holding the fully laden box in both flippers. It was no easy task to hoist the box of fish into the lifeboat and let it drop, before climbing in himself. He was glad that the mighty clatter that he had made hadn't alerted any of the crew.

He slumped down in the corner rather pleased with himself, thinking what an inspired piece of shopping he had just performed.

This was going to be the best meal ever!

The next morning, Parjiter could hardly move after munching his way through the entire box of fish. He realised that he had been just a little bit too greedy the night before.

However, at least he now knew where all his future meals were going to come from for the whole duration of the voyage, so this left him a rather contented and smug little penguin – and the humans didn't even know that he was there!

As the days passed and the ship sailed into a warmer climate, Parjiter was becoming rather uncomfortable with the rising temperature.

The ship had, by now, sailed passed the entire length of the country of Chile, then Peru and had now reached Ecuador. As they approached equatorial waters, he knew that he couldn't stay cooped up in his lifeboat for much longer due to the excessive heat. Parjiter needed to cool down and fast. It didn't, however, take him long to come to a decision.

What if I can find a quiet corner in that giant fridge, where I can stay hidden and just eat and sleep there until the outside temperature cools down sufficiently to move back into the safety of the lifeboat? he thought.

"Yep. Great idea! That's exactly what I'll do," he said to himself proudly.

After a couple of weeks had elapsed on the Pacific Ocean since the expedition had started, Parjiter suddenly heard a lot of excited voices coming from the deck of the ship. He ventured a look outside from the confines of his temporary accommodation to see what all the fuss was about, and was taken aback at the sight which met his eyes.

As there had been no land in sight for all that time, the ship, having now passed by the country of Colombia on the northwest of South America, entered a narrow stretch of water – the Panama Canal, where land was now clearly visible on both sides. This gave the crew some welcome reassurance that they were definitely heading in the right direction.

After passing through this channel and entering into the Caribbean Sea, it was just a relatively short journey until the research ship reached the wide-open expanse of the mighty North Atlantic Ocean, which would take them on the final part of their voyage.

It was still very warm outside, so Parjiter wouldn't be able to move out of the giant refrigerator just yet, but hopefully, it wouldn't be too long before he would be nearing the end of his long journey.

As the days passed, Parjiter could finally feel the outside temperature cooling down which indicated to him that the Arctic wasn't far off, and he could also now move back into the familiar surroundings of the lifeboat that he had come to regard as his second home.

Finally, after thirty-two days at sea and having travelled nearly 8,000 miles, the expedition ship slowly and majestically glided into the calm and icy waters of the southern tip of Greenland.

Their final destination was the small settlement of Nanortalik, the southernmost town in the massive island country of Greenland.

Parjiter thought, Finally we've arrived after all this time.

He surveyed the tranquil scene. He could see the odd iceberg floating in the sea, and it was certainly cold, although not as cold as the temperatures he was used to in the Antarctic.

He hoped that he was in the right place; however, he needn't have worried, as he overheard the leader of the scientific expedition saying to his colleagues, "Well, here we are at last. It's a small town, but the name Nanortalik in the Greenlandic language actually means 'Place of Polar Bears'."

Parjiter's heartbeat quickened.

"Well, I'm definitely in the right place. Now I just have to find some polar bears," he said confidently. With that thought in mind, he dived from the ship into the sea and swam ashore, before waddling off to explore this strange new land.

Chapter 5
A New Friend Awaits

Parjiter had never seen a place like this before. It was actual land and not just the sea ice that he had become used to. All the wooden houses in this small settlement were painted in an array of bright colours. It was a very welcoming sight.

He waddled through this little town; however, he hadn't spotted any of its inhabitants. Most of them had already taken to their fishing boats as selling fish was this community's main livelihood.

As he reached the end of the town, Parjiter wandered out on to the snow-covered terrain by the seashore and sat down for a rest. He felt very tired after his long journey, so he lay back on a mound of snow and quickly settled into a deep sleep.

After some time had elapsed, Parjiter was awakened suddenly. Something strange was happening. The mound of snow that he had been sleeping on began to move and seemed to be growing bigger and bigger.

Parjiter was confused at first, but he began to slowly realise that what he had been sleeping on wasn't a mound of snow at all. It was a sleeping polar bear who had been awoken from his slumbers and was now towering over him and staring down angrily, clearly not impressed that he had been disturbed from his afternoon nap.

Parjiter was terrified, but he felt that he was obliged to say something.

"Who are you?" he spluttered, nervously.

"What are you?" came the booming reply.

Parjiter realised that the polar bear would have never seen a penguin before, and he seemed rather taken aback at the sight of this funny little creature that had awoken him from his sleep.

"I'm a penguin," Parjiter started. "I don't actually live here. I came a long way from the other end of the world just to see a polar bear – which, of course, is the most wonderfully magnificent animal that has walked this earth EVER," he added emphatically.

This flattery didn't appear to be having much effect on the bear, who continued to stare down expressionless, still rather confused at the sight that had greeted his sleepy eyes.

Parjiter rambled on, "Sorry, if I woke you. I didn't mean to," and rather meekly asked, "Are you going to eat me?"

There was a moment of awkward silence.

"Eat you! Why would I do that? I don't even know what you are. You might taste horrible," said the bear. "The last thing I want is an upset tummy by eating something that disagrees with my digestive system."

"Yes, you're probably right. I couldn't agree more. I think that I would definitely taste horrible," Parjiter said, hurriedly continuing the conversation. "I'm actually a bird from the Antarctic, and I came here on a ship."

"Well, if you're a bird, why didn't you just fly here?" asked the bear.

"Because I can't fly," replied Parjiter.

"Can't fly! A bird that can't fly!" The bear burst into

laughter. "Well, why have you got wings if you can't fly?"

"Oh, these wings aren't for flying, they're for swimming. We penguins use them as flippers to propel ourselves through the water."

Parjiter was starting to feel a bit more at ease now. It seemed that the polar bear wasn't interested in eating him after all.

"My name is Parjiter Penguin. How do you do?" Parjiter tentatively offered an outstretched flipper which the bear grasped in his gigantic paw.

"My name," said the bear grandly, "is Bridgeforth Bear the Third!"

"Goodness, that's even longer than my name," said Parjiter. "You can call me Parjy for short. That's what all my friends call me. Can I call you Bridgy?"

"Certainly NOT!" said Bridgeforth sternly. "That just sounds common. I'll allow you to call me Bridgeforth. And just so we're clear, I shall call you Parjiter, NOT Parjy," he scoffed.

Parjiter was certainly not going to argue the point, so he readily agreed on how they were going to address each other from now on.

"So, how did you get your rather splendid name?" asked Parjiter curiously.

"Well, it's a bit of long story," Bridgeforth explained. "Many years ago, my great-grandfather lived in a zoo in a beautiful country called Scotland, and it was decided that he would be taken back home to be set free in the Arctic. So he was transported to a ship which was leaving from a big river called the Firth of Forth, which flows into the sea. To get to the sea, the ship had to pass under a huge bridge called the Forth Bridge. My great-grandfather was so impressed by this magnificent bridge that, years later, when his cub was born, he wanted to call him Forth Bridge.

"My great-grandmother told him, 'You can't call a bear Forth Bridge. Why don't we swap the name around and call him Bridge Forth, which we'll join together as just one name – Bridgeforth.'

"And so," the bear concluded, "my grandfather was named Bridgeforth Bear; my father was named Bridgeforth Bear the Second; and I became Bridgeforth Bear the Third."

"Wow," said Parjiter, "that's a very impressive story. No wonder you want to be called by your proper name. I'll bet no other bear is called Bridgeforth, and come to think of it, I don't think any other penguin is called Parjiter, so I suppose that makes us both rather special."

Bridgeforth nodded in agreement, and they both wandered off through the snow, chatting away to each other and learning about how each survived at opposite ends of the world.

After the new friends had been walking and exchanging stories for a while, they sat down at the edge of the sea ice, staring into the clear water.

"I'm hungry," stated Bridgeforth.

"What do polar bears eat?" enquired Parjiter.

"Well, all my friends and family catch seals and eat them for their meals," Bridgeforth replied.

"Wow! You eat seals? Back where I come from, it's the seals that eat us," Parjiter said with a shudder.

"Well," said Bridgeforth, "I'm not really that keen on seals, to be honest – too much blubber on them for my liking, but we need blubber to store us up for the winter. Personally, I prefer fish, but I'm usually too slow to catch them. We're good swimmers, us polar bears, but we're not very fast in the water. I actually think that the fish just laugh at us when we try to catch them."

Parjiter stifled a snigger to himself and said, "Penguins are good swimmers, and we're also very fast. We can dive up to 1,800 feet and hold our breath for about twenty minutes, so we have no problem in catching fish."

Bridgeforth was very impressed. "I don't suppose you could catch some for me, could you?" he asked.

"Yeah, no problem. Now you'll see just how useful our flippers are for speeding through the water."

And with that, Parjiter dived into the sea.

Bridgeforth's jaw dropped in astonishment as Parjiter flashed through the water. "He's even faster than the fish," he said to himself.

After just a couple of minutes, Parjiter appeared with a beak-full of fish and dropped them beside Bridgeforth.

"I'll bet you've got a big appetite, Bridgeforth," said Parjiter, "so I'll catch some more fish for you."

Bridgeforth didn't reply as he was too busy munching the first batch of fish that Parjiter had supplied.

Several fishing trips later, Bridgeforth lay back on the ice, having gorged himself so much that he couldn't eat any more.

"I'll make one last trip," said Parjiter, "so that I can have my dinner too."

Bridgeforth nodded contentedly and watched as Parjiter disappeared into the sea once more.

Several minutes had elapsed without Parjiter reappearing, and Bridgeforth thought to himself, I know Parjiter said that Emperor Penguins can hold their breaths for twenty minutes, but this is the longest that he's been under the water.

He was now starting to get a bit worried that something may have happened to his friend.

Just then, there was a disturbance in the sea beside him, and Parjiter suddenly propelled himself out of the water and on to the ice, quickly pursued by a hungry seal. The seal had been chasing Parjiter for about ten minutes, and now moved towards him with its jaws open.

A large shadow gradually appeared over the seal, however, and on looking up, the seal was so alarmed at the sight of Bridgeforth baring his teeth and snarling menacingly, that it slinked and slithered back off the ice shelf and into the sea, disappearing into the depths of the clear blue water.

Parjiter's heart was racing, and he breathlessly thanked his pal for saving his life.

"That's what friends are for," said Bridgeforth with a triumphant look on his face. "You supply me with plenty of fish for my dinner, and I'll protect you from hungry seals. Deal?"

"Deal," said Parjiter gratefully.

Bridgeforth realised that Parjiter hadn't actually eaten anything himself yet as he was, no doubt, too preoccupied in ensuring that he wasn't going to end up as the seal's next meal.

"Are you going to catch some fish for your own dinner now?" Bridgeforth asked.

"Not just now," Parjiter replied slowly. "I seem to have lost my appetite."

Chapter 6
A Wake-Up Call to the World

Over the next few days, the mealtime routine remained the same. Parjiter would catch enough fish for both of them, and Bridgeforth would stand guard on the edge of the sea ice to ensure that his friend avoided any more life-threatening encounters.

As the snow began to fall heavily, Parjiter demonstrated to Bridgeforth the game that he played with his friends back home in the Antarctic when they came across similar conditions.

He climbed slowly to the top of a nearby mound and proceeded to flop down on his belly and propel himself down the slope using his flippers and feet.

Bridgeforth thought that this game looked rather cool, so he decided that he would give it a go. At the top of the snow-covered mound, he too flopped down on to his belly as Parjiter had done, and he pushed himself forward down the hill.

However, he lost his balance halfway down, and instead of sliding to a halt, he somersaulted uncontrollably to the base of the mound and landed unceremoniously with a thud, his face covered in snow.

The sight of a bear resembling a giant snowball produced howls of laughter from Parjiter, and after Bridgeforth had composed himself, he too saw the funny side and joined in the hilarity.

At the end of an exhausting day, the two friends collapsed on to the soft snow and chatted breathlessly, gazing up at the star-filled sky.

Far away on the distant horizon, a curious green light could be seen. Then red and blue lights appeared. They sped across the night sky until it was awash with colour, dancing high above the companions like a multi-coloured billowing sheet. The luminous green light, in particular, was a spectacular sight to behold.

Bridgeforth had seen this light show before.

"That's the aurora borealis, or northern lights, as we call them. I never get tired of seeing that. It just makes me feel so relaxed."

"Me too, Bridgeforth," said Parjiter. "We get these lights, too, in the Antarctic. Down there, they're called the aurora australis or southern lights. You can almost feel yourself being hypnotised by the beautiful colours."

Once the light show had passed, the two pals drifted off to sleep, in readiness for what was to be a very tough day ahead.

Parjiter didn't know it, but tomorrow was when Bridgeforth knew that he would have to part company with his new friend. The time had come for him to start his long journey even further north, as he had previously arranged to meet up with a large group of polar bears who would be travelling to the meeting point from all different directions.

They would then be working as one large team with the sole purpose of hunting seals, whose blubber they would need to sustain them in readiness for the harsh winter months to come.

As dawn arrived, Bridgeforth broke the news to his

friend. Parjiter asked, "Why do you have to travel so far north to stock up on your winter food supplies? Can you not just catch what you need here?"

Bridgeforth answered, "I wish we could, but we need to dig holes in the thick ice to reach the sea underneath so that it makes hunting easier for us. The seals use them as breathing holes and we can catch them unawares. We can't do that down here as the ice is melting, which means that we would lose the element of surprise, as any seals that we were hunting would see us first and would escape into the sea. That means we'd go hungry. Also, the more that the ice gradually melts, the further north we have to go to survive."

"But why is the ice melting here?" asked Parjiter.

"Well, that's why all the scientific researchers are up here – to study the changing environment," replied Bridgeforth.

"Yes, we have them, too, in the Antarctic. It was one of their ships that I stowed away on to get here," said Parjiter.

"It seems," Bridgeforth continued, "that most of the problem is directly caused by humans themselves. From what I've heard, the humans all over the world burn too much coal, gas and oil – which they call fossil fuels – for their energy, and that releases poisonous gases into the air which can't escape and so increases the air temperature. As the air temperature increases, it melts the polar ice caps, breaks up the massive glaciers that you can see around us and causes global warming. So us polar bears are having to move further and further north to survive. If this was to continue, then it might not be too long before all of the polar bear population could eventually die off and become extinct," he concluded, shaking his head in despair.

"Oh, my goodness, Bridgeforth, that's terrible! I didn't realise that things were so bad," said Parjiter, who hated the thought of there being no polar bears left on the planet.

"Can't the humans see what's happening to your home and stop using these fossil fuels?" asked Parjiter in desperation.

"Well, only if the humans across the world start listening to the scientists and use energy from the wind and the sun, instead, as many of them are apparently starting to do."

"But there is hope," Bridgeforth said optimistically. "Apparently, there are more and more young humans all over the world who are trying to change things. Hopefully, they'll manage to do that before it's too late."

Bridgeforth could see that Parjiter was very worried about this whole situation.

"Cheer up," said Bridgeforth with a smile. "We must have faith in the young people of the world. I'm sure that they will make a difference and eventually change things for the better."

"Now," said Bridgeforth, deliberately changing the subject, "I've got a long walk ahead of me which will take several days, so you'll have to make sure that I have a big meal of fresh fish to keep my energy levels up."

"No!" said Parjiter.

"No?" Bridgeforth responded in surprise.

"No. Unless, of course, you let me come with you, in which case, I'll catch you as many fish as you want," stated Parjiter.

"But you'll never be able to keep up with me. Your legs are too short!"

"Well," said Parjiter, with a huge grin on his face, "I could get a lift on your back. I'm not very heavy, so you would hardly notice the difference. Besides, you'd have some company for your journey."

Bridgeforth thought for a few seconds then conceded, "Okay, you win. We'll go on the journey together."

"Yesss!" said Parjiter, punching the air with his flipper. "I'll catch us the best fish you've ever tasted and as much as you can eat!"

Chapter 7
The Long Trek North

"Ready?" asked Bridgeforth.

"Ready!" replied Parjiter excitedly.

"Then let's get started. Jump on my back and hold on tight."

The companions set off on their epic journey, Bridgeforth steadily plodding through the snow and Parjiter, with his feet up and flippers clasped behind his head, relaxing and laying back on this big, furry moving blanket.

This is the way to travel, thought Parjiter, with a contented smile on his face.

"So, how far are we going?" asked Parjiter.

"Well," replied Bridgeforth, "probably a lot further than you were thinking – about two hundred miles."

Parjiter sat up abruptly. "Two hundred miles! Are you serious?" he exclaimed in disbelief. "How long is that going to take us?"

"Could be the best part of two weeks, depending on the weather. Snowstorms could slow us down, so we'll just have to hope that we're lucky," explained Bridgeforth.

"Are you sure you know the way?" enquired Parjiter. "I hope you don't get us lost."

"Don't worry, I've made this journey before. We'll make sure that the sea is always on our right, so we know that we're travelling in the right direction."

Bridgeforth seemed to have everything worked out.

A thought suddenly crossed Parjiter's mind, and he said to Bridgeforth, "I've just remembered! I can only stay here in the Arctic for a month, as I have to go back home when the expedition ship leaves again for the Antarctic."

"It's been four days since I met you on my first day here," he continued, "so if we're travelling for about two weeks, and then you have to hunt for a few days for your winter supplies, that's not going to leave me enough time to make the journey back to where the ship is docked."

Parjiter started to panic. If he missed the ship, he would be stranded in the Arctic for good, and would never see his home again.

"Don't you worry about that," Bridgeforth said calmly. "I'll get you back in time."

"But how?" Parjiter continued.

Bridgeforth smiled. "You leave that to me. I've got all that worked out, and I can tell you this, it'll be less tiring and much quicker than the journey up there."

"Well, if you say so."

Parjiter started to relax. He felt that he could trust Bridgeforth, so he lay down again on his big friend's back, as he plodded steadily through the snow-covered ice sheet.

Darkness was beginning to fall quickly. Bridgeforth stopped and said, "Okay, we'll camp here for the night. We'll need some fish to eat to keep our energy levels up— correction, my energy levels, I should say, as I've been doing all the walking!"

Parjiter couldn't exactly disagree with that.

"No problem," said Parjiter. "You've kept us near the sea, so I'll go and catch us some nice tasty fish."

"Okay. I'll dig us a shelter in the snow to sleep in, and

for goodness' sake, Parjiter, keep an eye out for seals!" Bridgeforth stated emphatically.

"Oh, don't worry about that. I've learned my lesson," retorted Parjiter, as he waddled down to the water's edge and disappeared beneath the surface of the waves.

Parjiter made several trips, his beak laden with fish after each successful foray into the sea.

Bridgeforth had completed the shelter, and after stuffing themselves with fish, the two of them settled down for the night for a well-earned rest.

The following morning, they set off again on the next leg of their journey. They followed the same routine, as their long trek progressed, with Parjiter providing the meals, and Bridgeforth providing the transport.

There was little variation in the snowscape, with the undulating hard-packed snow and ice all around them and the reassuring sight of the sea to their right.

After a few days into their monotonous journey, Parjiter spotted a strange structure in the distance. As the pair slowly got closer, Parjiter could make out a manmade building with what looked like a giant sock perched on top of a mast and billowing in the wind.

"Well, that's a bit random," Parjiter said to Bridgeforth. "What on earth is that?"

Bridgeforth replied, with a satisfied smile on his face, "That, my friend, is a weather station. It's stuck in the middle of nowhere, really, but the scientists seem to think it's useful. It's certainly useful to me, though, because I always pass it on my trip north, so when I see it, I know that I'm heading in the right direction."

Bridgeforth continued, "I also know that we're now about halfway towards my meeting place with the other polar bears."

As they passed by the weather station and gradually left it in the distance, Bridgeforth knew that the further north they travelled, the worse the weather was likely to become, but there was no point in worrying Parjiter with this information, so he kept it to himself, at least until Parjiter noticed the change in the weather conditions himself.

Another two days passed as Bridgeforth steadily continued on his way, Parjiter noticing that the huge footprints that his friend was leaving in the snow were becoming progressively deeper.

The wind speed had gradually increased, until it had now reached gale force, and this, combined with the heavy snow that was falling, resulted in very treacherous blizzard conditions. As the visibility was now almost zero and with the light fading fast, Bridgeforth made the decision to stop for the night.

Parjiter said, "I better get us some fish before we bed down for the night."

"No! Absolutely not," retorted Bridgeforth. "It's far too dangerous. You can't even see the water's edge because of the blizzard. You'd get confused about the direction you were going in and would get completely lost in no time at all. We can do without food tonight, and you can catch some fish in the morning if the weather improves." And with that plan made perfectly clear, Bridgeforth proceeded to burrow out a snow cave as shelter from the worsening weather conditions.

Bridgeforth was an expert on survival due to his past experience of coping with the perils of blizzards, whereas, back home, Parjiter had relied on thousands of penguins circling around in a gigantic huddle to combat these types of conditions, with a rotation system in operation. This system allowed the penguins on the outside to gradually move into the centre, so that they could all take turns of keeping warm.

Bridgeforth snuggled into the snow cave that he had created, and before long, he had settled into a deep sleep coupled with the loudest snoring that Parjiter had ever heard.

Chapter 8
A Terrifying Ordeal

Parjiter thought to himself that it was a shame that his friend had to go without his daily meal of fresh fish. After all, he was the one doing all the hard work and needed to eat to keep up his strength. It would be a nice surprise, Parjiter decided, if he went fishing now whilst Bridgeforth was asleep, and then presented him with a readymade breakfast when he woke up.

As for the possibility of getting lost, well, all he had to do was to keep listening out for Bridgeforth's snoring, and he would follow the sound of the snores on his way back with the catch.

Parjiter thought that this was a brilliant idea, so he headed off into the blizzard, which was so strong now that it took all of his strength to force himself forward, in the direction of what he thought was the water's edge at the end of the ice sheet.

Suddenly, and without warning, there was a shuddering bang which stopped Parjiter in his tracks. He had never heard anything that loud before. This was followed by a series of ear-splitting cracks.

The weather had become so severe that a huge section of the ice sheet had split, and Parjiter felt the ice moving beneath his feet. This great mass then started to tip up, and Parjiter began to slowly slide down the icy slope towards a gaping crevasse that had opened up.

The more that he tried frantically to grip the ice, the more he kept sliding towards this massive gap, which seemed would inevitably swallow him up.

Parjiter was yelling for help, but his voice was just being carried away on the ever-strengthening wind. The situation seemed hopeless. He was spinning uncontrollably towards the crevasse, until his feet now dangled over the edge. He closed his eyes and waited for the inevitable drop that would take him into the depths of this gigantic hole in the ice.

At that moment, Parjiter felt a sudden pressure on his flipper, which was pinning him to the side of the fractured ice. His feet were still dangling over the edge, but strangely, he wasn't falling, and he couldn't understand why, until he looked up and saw what was preventing his drop into oblivion.

A huge bear paw had stopped his fall and was now pulling him up and out of the deep chasm.

Bridgeforth had been woken up by the sound of the cracking ice and had seen that his friend was missing, and so, he left the safety of his shelter to look for him. Thankfully, he saw what was happening and quickly assessed the danger. His claws were able to grip the ice and prevent him from sliding, and that had enabled him to grasp Parjiter by his flipper and haul him to safety.

Parjiter was too shocked to be able to say anything, but felt so thankful that his big pal had saved him and was now carrying him back to the relative safety of the snow cave.

When Parjiter was finally able to speak, he said weakly and by way of explanation, "I thought I'd surprise you by catching fish for breakfast."

"Well, you certainly surprised me, but not, I think, in the way that you had intended. Please don't do anything like that again though!" Bridgeforth said, with a huge degree of relief in his voice.

"I won't," said Parjiter apologetically. "I just wasn't expecting half of the Arctic to suddenly disappear under my feet."

Bridgeforth smiled. "A bit of an exaggeration there Parjiter; but in the Arctic, you have to expect the unexpected."

The two pals lay back in the snow cave, reflecting in silence on the close escape they'd just had, and then gradually drifted off into an uneasy sleep, brought on by the exertions of the terrifying trauma they had just encountered.

As dawn broke, the wind and the snow had subsided sufficiently to allow a clear view of their route ahead.

Bridgeforth and Parjiter rose slowly from their makeshift shelter and surveyed the damage to the ice sheet that had been caused by the previous night's storm.

Several hundred metres of ice had been ripped up, and the pair were able to see the full extent of the damage.

A shiver ran down Parjiter's spine as he looked down into the crevasse and momentarily thought what might have been, had his big pal not been around to pull him to safety.

Bridgeforth interrupted his friend's thoughts.

"Well, that's twice I've saved your life now – once from the seal, and now from that huge crevasse in the ice sheet. I think you owe me an extra special breakfast." He grinned. "Are you up for it?"

Parjiter replied, "You bet I'm up for it. I'm going to catch you the best breakfast you've ever had." And with these words echoing in Bridgeforth's ears, Parjiter dived into the sea and several trips later had laid out an impressive variety of fresh fish on the snow.

Bridgeforth was delighted with this extra-special meal, and they both munched their way through the whole array of fare on offer from this well-presented gourmet platter.

Bridgeforth felt invigorated after this feast and was ready to take on the challenges that a new day had to offer, secure in the knowledge that, from past experience, the remainder of the journey should be fairly straightforward.

"Okay, let's go," stated Bridgeforth. "We'll have to take a detour around that huge crack in the ice shelf and then get back on track."

Parjiter jumped on to his friend's back, and they set off on the final stage of their journey, surveying the damaged ice shelf as they passed by and peering into the depths of what seemed to be this bottomless chasm.

Chapter 9

A Polar Bear Convention

The next couple of days were largely uneventful and passed by quickly.

"We're almost there," said Bridgeforth, with a measure of anticipation in his voice. "The meeting place for all my fellow polar bears should be just over the top of this ridge in front of us."

After two weeks of exhausting travel, Bridgeforth made his final ascent, and peering over the top of the snow-covered mound down into the valley below, he was greeted by the sight of about twenty polar bears milling about and chatting to one another about the trials encountered on their respective journeys.

Bridgeforth smiled to himself in quiet satisfaction.

"I'll build you a snow shelter up here," he said quietly to his companion. "I don't think it would be a good idea for you to come with me any further, with all those hungry polar bears down there."

"For once," said Parjiter in agreement, "I'm definitely taking your advice. There's no way I'm going to risk taking a step further, in case your friends suddenly develop a taste for penguin pie."

Bridgeforth nodded in acknowledgement. "The sea is just over there to your right, so you can catch enough fish for yourself, then get back to the shelter unseen. I'll be away for two or three days at most, hunting seals, so for goodness' sake, keep out of sight until then."

Parjiter watched as Bridgeforth made his way down the

slope to be greeted enthusiastically by his old friends. He thought to himself, smiling, that Bridgeforth fully deserved to have lots of friends. He was, after all, a very special bear.

Over the next three days, there was frantic activity down on the ice shelf where several ice holes were being manufactured for the purpose of luring any unsuspecting seals who had been swimming in the sea beneath the ice. Those who were in need of a break in the ice to come up for air would then be pounced upon by the hungry polar bears who were lying in wait.

If the polar bears were to survive through the winter, it was essential for them to consume the blubber from the captured seals, which would fatten them up and help to sustain them for the long months ahead.

Parjiter watched all this activity from afar, and although fascinated, he was glad that he was confined to a place of relative safety, perched on top of the snow mound, within easy reach of the snow-cave shelter which housed his supply of freshly caught fish.

At the end of the third day that Bridgeforth had been away, Parjiter could hear a bit of a commotion which was coming from down in the valley below him.

As he peered over the top of the mound to investigate this disturbance, he could clearly see all the polar bears congratulating each other on a successful hunting expedition. They had all worked well together as a team and, as a result, had managed to capture and consume a sufficient number of seals which would set them up perfectly for the winter.

With their mission accomplished, the community of bears said their farewells and set off in different directions back to where they had come from.

One polar bear made his way up the slope towards Parjiter. A momentary state of panic quickly subsided when he thankfully recognised the bear in question to be his friend, Bridgeforth.

"Well, you managed to keep out of trouble then, eh! Wonders will never cease," said a rather bloated Bridgeforth.

"I see you've not exactly been on a diet," retorted Parjiter, with a smirk on his face. "Looks like you're well stoked up for the winter," he said, as he pointed his flipper towards Bridgeforth's rather expanded waistline.

"Well, that was the purpose of the exercise. Job done!" replied a very satisfied bear.

"Now," said Parjiter, changing the topic of conversation completely, "the research ship that I arrived on will be leaving in a week. It took us two weeks to get here, so what's this big plan of yours to get me back in time before it leaves?"

"Ah," replied Bridgeforth, with a smug smile on his face, "follow me and I'll show you."

The pair wandered down to the water's edge and sat down.

"Tell me," said Bridgeforth, with an air of authority, "look out to sea. What do you see?"

Parjiter gazed out on to the wide expanse of the ice-cold blue waters.

"Nothing." Parjiter shrugged.

"Look a bit closer to the shore," Bridgeforth continued.

"Still nothing really. Just a few broken bits of the ice shelf floating past," replied Parjiter.

"Exactly," said Bridgeforth. "They're as regular as clockwork and all different sizes too. And they all flow in the same direction – south."

Bridgeforth continued with his explanation. "The currents from the Arctic Ocean take all the broken pieces of ice shelf, or ice floes as they're called, and transport them down through the Greenland Sea, into the Denmark Strait, and continue into the North Atlantic Ocean – in other words, back down the same coastline that we kept in sight on the way up here.

"Finally, the ocean currents split as we approach the southern tip of Greenland. We just have to make sure that we keep hugging the coastline into Nanortalik, by changing ice floes, if necessary, until we arrive at the place where your ship is docked."

Bridgeforth was on a roll now, with his master plan.

"All we have to do now is wait for a suitable-sized ice floe – the larger the better due to my rather increased size – and jump on it. Then sit back and relax and let the ocean current do the rest. It'll be much quicker than our journey up here, as we'll be moving all the time, so we won't have to stop for the night.

"You can just dive off the ice floe to catch some fish on the way, when we get hungry, and we'll be back in plenty of time to catch your ship before it leaves for your journey home."

Bridgeforth sat back and waited for a response once

all this information had sunk in. It wasn't long before the expected response was forthcoming.

"Wow!" exclaimed Parjiter. "That is absolutely amazing. You've really got all of this worked out perfectly, haven't you? Got to say, big buddy, I'm well impressed!"

"Just a bit of forward planning," said Bridgeforth, feeling rather pleased with himself.

Several broken slabs of ice shelf had drifted past, until Bridgeforth pointed purposefully out to sea.

"Look, this one coming up now; it's a perfect size. Definitely big enough to take both of us comfortably – and it's thick enough not to break up on the journey back."

The two friends swam out to the ice floe as it drifted nearer and then scrambled up on to its surface. They placed themselves in the middle to ensure there was perfect weight distribution, and then just lay back, watching the sea lapping around the edges of what was to be their own personal mode of transport for the next few days.

Chapter 10
A Race Against Time

As the Arctic current acted as a conveyor belt for the myriad of ice floes that populated the coastal waters, Parjiter marvelled at how the weather could change so rapidly from one extreme to the other.

Just a few days ago they were battling against a ferocious blizzard, but now the sea was calm and the sun was glinting off the array of broken ice sheet pieces that were travelling south at an idyllic but steady pace.

After all the hard work and exertions that Bridgeforth previously had to endure on the long walk north, it was now his turn to rest, and let Parjiter periodically dive off the ice floe and supply the pair with fresh fish, which they could consume at their leisure.

The sea, thankfully, had remained calm for the first three days into their return journey. As he was idly surveying the shoreline, Parjiter spotted a familiar sight.

"Look, Bridgeforth!" he exclaimed excitedly. "We're passing the weather station with that funny looking wind sock thing. That must mean that we're halfway back to the ship already."

"Yep, we're right on schedule to have you back in Nanortalik in plenty of time," replied Bridgeforth, lazily.

Another day had passed without incident, when Bridgeforth noticed out of the corner of his eye a massive object off to their left, which had been drifting on an adjacent ocean current further out to sea, and whose momentum was now carrying it towards the sheet of ice occupied by the two friends.

Bridgeforth realised only too well that the object in question was a gigantic iceberg, and the nearer that it approached them, the more obvious it became that it was on a direct collision course with their ice floe.

There was nothing that they could do to halt its relentless progress, so Bridgeforth and Parjiter had to brace themselves for the impact.

The iceberg smashed into the ice floe with a shuddering jolt, splintering their erstwhile trusty transport into so many little pieces, that it now resembled piles of confetti strewn across the suddenly churned up waters next to the shoreline.

As it was clear that they would now be forced to curtail their journey, they swam ashore so that they could weigh up the situation in which they now found themselves.

"Well," said Bridgeforth, "it's like I said before – you've got to expect the unexpected. Just when you think everything is going smoothly..." His voice tailed off as he shook his head in reluctant acceptance of their bad luck.

"So, what now?" asked Parjiter. "Do we wait for another ice floe to come by?"

"I don't think that we can afford to do that. If we wait, and a suitable sized ice floe doesn't arrive, we'll have wasted time that we haven't got. We'll have to walk the rest of the way," Bridgeforth announced. "There's no alternative."

"But is that going to leave us enough time to get back to the ship before it sails?" asked Parjiter, anxiously.

"It'll be touch and go, so we'd better start now. We've got three days to complete the journey. Jump on my back and let's get moving," said Bridgeforth forcefully. "We haven't got a moment to lose."

Luckily, the weather remained calm and the underfoot conditions were fairly smooth, so that Bridgeforth was able to move at a relatively brisk pace.

To Parjiter's surprise, Bridgeforth, on occasion, broke into a run, which meant that he had to hold on tightly to his big companion to prevent him from being thrown off.

Polar bears can move surprisingly quickly, up to about 25 miles per hour, but only in short bursts. Then they have to slow down again to conserve energy.

Parjiter was so grateful to his new best friend for the sheer effort that he was making in trying to get him back to where the ship was docked. Bridgeforth always seemed to be able to take control of any situation which arose and deal with it in the most efficient manner.

The pair travelled for most of the day and slept for only a few hours at night, with Parjiter supplying the supper. On the second night after their unfortunate mishap, the aurora borealis appeared in the sky again, but instead of admiring its beauty, this time they used it as extra light which enabled them to keep travelling for an extra few miles, before having to stop for a curtailed sleep when complete darkness descended.

The friends rose early the next morning. This was the last day before the expedition ship was due to set off on the return trip back to Parjiter's homeland in the Antarctic.

The final leg of their journey saw Bridgeforth break into periodic running which had resulted in him becoming

increasingly exhausted with the effort that he had been expending. He had now almost reached a standstill, when over the next ridge, he spotted the small town of Nanortalik in the distance.

They had finally completed their journey. Now it was just a matter of ensuring that Parjiter could slip back on to the ship unseen.

As they approached the outskirts of the town, Bridgeforth rounded the final ridge which would take him to the dockside, but to Parjiter's horror, he saw the ship slowly making its way out of the harbour.

"Oh no!" exclaimed Parjiter. "We're too late."

Bridgeforth hurriedly looked around and spotted a headland that the ship would have to pass by before it reached the open sea.

"Quick," he said, "get back up on to my back and hang on tight." And with that, he summoned up one final effort and raced towards the headland as fast as he could run. "I think that I can make it before the ship gets there," he spluttered.

Bridgeforth drew to a halt, exhausted, having reached the headland just ahead of the ship arriving there, and breathlessly said to his pal, "The ship's just approaching now. You're a good swimmer, so if you swim out to the ship as fast as you can, you can propel yourself out of the water and through one of the lower portholes."

Parjiter turned, gave his friend a huge hug and thanked him for everything that he had done for him over the month that they had known each other.

"You never know," said Bridgeforth, "I might even find a way to come and visit you in the Antarctic. Now wouldn't that be something?" He grinned.

"It really would," agreed Parjiter. "I'd love to meet up with you again sometime, and I could show you around where I live."

"Well, it's been a pleasure making your acquaintance, Parjiter Penguin," said Bridgeforth in a mockingly formal tone, as he extended a huge paw towards his friend.

Parjiter grasped the outstretched paw in his flippers, shaking it vigorously and replying in a similar tone, "The pleasure has been all mine, Bridgeforth Bear the Third."

Bridgeforth chuckled. "Now, you'd better get going; the ship's nearly here."

And with these final words, Parjiter dived into the sea and darted through the water at great speed, just beneath the surface.

Bridgeforth stood on the headland watching the gently undulating waves, when suddenly, in the distance, he caught sight of Parjiter propelling himself out of the water and, with pinpoint accuracy, disappearing through one of the lower portholes to the stern of the ship.

The research ship steamed past the headland. As Bridgeforth stood watching as it made its way into open water, he noticed that a small figure had appeared at the stern, frantically waving a flipper to his best pal.

Bridgeforth raised a giant paw and waved back, as the ship continued to sail on.

Parjiter watched as his big friend on the shoreline

seemed to get smaller and smaller, as the ship moved further away; and as Bridgeforth finally disappeared from sight, Parjiter felt an overwhelming feeling of sadness, as the realisation struck home that they would, in all probability, never meet again.

Chapter 11
A Triumphant Return

Parjiter sat back against the wooden slats at the ship's stern and reflected upon the events that had taken place over the last month, shaking his head slowly in disbelief, that so much could have happened in such a relatively short space of time; and how his new friend had saved his life, not once but twice.

He felt that the month-long journey that now lay ahead of him, which would signal his return to the Antarctic, was really going to drag, in sharp contrast to the previous month that had just flown by.

"Right," said Parjiter, snapping himself out of his innermost thoughts, "I'd better check that everything here is still in the same place as before."

First things first, though. He had to make sure that the giant refrigerator was still accessible. That was a priority.

The doors had again been left ajar, which was a good start, so that Parjiter was able to squeeze through.

He made his way directly to the back where the supplies of fish were kept, and to his relief, these supplies were stacked up in exactly the same position as before. He grabbed as much as he could carry and made his way to the lifeboat that had been his home on the way up to the Arctic.

Climbing precariously under the tarpaulin that was covering the top of the small boat, he settled down into the same part that he had previously occupied, depositing the fish in the corner, in readiness for when he would begin to feel hungry. It just wouldn't be the same, however, eating alone without the company of his big furry pal.

Parjiter, pretty much followed the same routine on the journey home, as he had done before, switching his living quarters to the giant refrigerator when the outside temperature became too warm; and then, after the ship had passed back through the Panama Canal and down past the equator, moving back into the lifeboat, when the air began to cool.

The journey had become extremely tedious as the ship entered the third week of the voyage home. However, from inside the shelter of his lifeboat, Parjiter could feel that the steady, monotonous sway of the vessel was gradually becoming more pronounced, until, without warning, he was suddenly thrown across the width of his hideaway.

The startled young penguin ventured a look from under the tarpaulin, only to be greeted by the sight of increasingly heavy seas which were being churned up by a howling gale.

The ship was now being uncontrollably thrown about on the angry ocean, very much akin to a seal being helplessly tossed about and tormented by a pod of killer whales. That was a disturbing sight that Parjiter had previously witnessed first-hand and not something of which he particularly wanted to be reminded.

These seas had now developed into the heaviest that he had ever encountered, and he was amazed that the ship was able to withstand the constant battering of wave after relentless wave.

The storm raged on for the rest of the day, before gradually subsiding to the extent that the ship, again, appeared to retake control of its own destiny. It ploughed on heroically through the great Pacific rollers until the end of the journey south became a reality.

The thing that had delighted Parjiter the most, though, was not that the storm had passed, but that he had survived it without becoming seasick – and it had been much worse than the heavy seas that he had encountered on his very first outing on this sea-faring vessel.

He felt a sense of pride about this fact, and now considered himself to be a fully-fledged sailor of the highest order.

The research ship rounded the southern tip of Chile, as it manoeuvred its way into Puerto Williams, where it unloaded part of its cargo, before continuing on up the Beagle Channel to Ushuaia, where the bulk of the heavy equipment was then unloaded.

The final part of this mammoth voyage was now underway, as the ship headed back out across the Drake Passage, ready to berth, back at its original starting point.

Parjiter broke from the cover of the lifeboat and made his way to the bow of the ship, where he saw a familiar sight.

His heart leapt as he recognised his own home ice shelf slowly coming into view. After three months on his great adventure, he was finally home.

As the ship berthed and dropped anchor, the sight that

greeted Parjiter left him open-mouthed and, for once, entirely speechless. He could hear the unmistakeable sound of cheering and the frantic clapping of flippers. He couldn't understand this at first as he had only told his friends about his planned adventure to the Arctic, but word must have spread, and now, what seemed like the whole penguin colony had turned out to welcome him home.

Parjiter, of course, was never one to pass up an opportunity like this, and so he climbed up on to the bow of the ship, posing briefly for effect, and proceeded to execute a spectacular dive into the sea. Emerging from the water and effortlessly jumping on to the shoreline, he was, befitting of his newly acquired superstar status, swamped by his friends, all excitedly bombarding him with questions.

Parjiter held up his flippers to quell the noise and announced to the assembled throng:

"The last three months have been the most incredible of my life. As the new school term starts tomorrow, I'll tell you all about it then, and especially about a great friend that I made up in the Arctic – a Polar Bear!"

There was a collective gasp.

"Friends with a polar bear?" queried one of the penguins.

"How is that possible?" enquired another.

"He must be delirious. Too much sun!" stated another.

The murmurs of disbelief reverberated around the cold Antarctic air, as the huddle of penguins gradually dispersed.

The following morning, Parjiter made his way to school, ready for the new term and bursting with enthusiasm, as he prepared to regale his fellow classmates with tales of his amazing Arctic adventure.

As he waddled along, a familiar voice interrupted his thoughts.

"Well, you've certainly been making a name for yourself Parjiter. That was a very reckless expedition that you embarked upon – but a very brave one," said a smiling Primrose Penguin. "We can't wait to hear all about it."

"You know, Miss Primrose," said Parjiter, "it all started with something you said."

"Really? I'm intrigued. Do tell," she said.

"Well, you said in your last lesson that a penguin and a polar bear could never meet. I think that I can now definitely put paid to that myth," stated Parjiter, emphatically.

Miss Primrose was impressed. "It looks like you'll be doing the teaching today then, Parjiter, and to mark the occasion, I've prepared a very special lunch."

"Don't tell me; let me guess," said Parjiter, "it wouldn't be fish pie by any chance, would it?"

"No, it's not, actually. It's my special recipe – krill and squid bake," announced Miss Primrose with pride.

Well, wonders will never cease, thought Parjiter, with a smile spreading across his face, as they both entered the classroom. This would be a presentation that no one would ever forget.

That night, as Parjiter lay back, trying to make sense of all the muddled thoughts churning about in his head, his gaze was drawn to the clear night sky, as an awe-inspiring light show came into view – the aurora australis.

A smile broke out on to his face as he remembered vividly, just a few short weeks previously, both he and his new friend Bridgeforth were looking up at the sky together and marvelling at the Arctic's equivalent – the aurora borealis.

It felt to Parjiter that Bridgeforth had somehow arranged this special show to personally welcome him home.

He wondered what Bridgeforth was doing now. Would he ever see his amazing big friend again? Would Bridgeforth figure out a way to travel down to the Antarctic to visit him? He was, after all, the most resourceful individual that he had ever met and the best friend that a penguin would be lucky enough to ever have.

Parjiter's eyes became heavy as an involuntary yawn escaped from his beak.

Would Bridgeforth surprise him and just turn up one day unannounced?

"Maybe one day," he mused, sleepily. "One day."

"Now," said Parjiter to himself, "what was it that Miss Primrose said to the class? Ah, yes, 'Polar bears and penguins can never meet.'"

"Really! Well, we'll see about that!"

THE END